This book belongs to...

....

....

Rapunzel

Once upon a time there lived a couple who after many years, found they were expecting a baby.

Their tiny cottage stood next to a river. Across the river was a beautiful garden full of glorious flowers and tasty-looking vegetables. One day, the woman looked across the river and saw a vegetable called rampion growing in the garden. It looked delicious, and she longed to taste it. She begged her husband to get some.

The garden belonged to an evil witch, and he refused. But his wife would eat nothing else, and grew thin and pale. At last he agreed.

That night, the man crossed the river, entered the witch's garden and picked handfuls of rampion. Suddenly the evil witch appeared. "How dare you steal from me!" she roared.

"F-Forgive me," the man stammered. "My wife is expecting a baby and longed for some of this vegetable. If she doesn't have it, I'm afraid she will die."

"Very well," said the witch, "take all you want. But you must give me something in return. When your baby is born, I must have it."

Terrified, the man agreed and fled.

The wife was overjoyed and made a salad with the rampion. She ate it hungrily.

After that, the man went to the witch's garden every day. He brought home baskets full of rampion for his wife, and she grew strong and healthy. A few months later she gave birth to a beautiful baby girl.

The man had forgotten all about his promise to the witch, but when the baby was just a day old, she burst in and took her away. The baby's parents were heartbroken and never saw her or the witch again.

The witch called the baby Rapunzel. She took her to a cottage deep in a forest, and took good care of her.

On Rapunzel's twelfth birthday, the witch imprisoned her in a forbidding high tower, with no doors and just one small window at the very top.

Every day the witch came and stood at the bottom of the tower, and called,
"Rapunzel, Rapunzel!
Let down your long hair!"

Rapunzel would let down her long, golden hair, and the witch would begin to climb up.

Rapunzel spent many lonely years in her tower. To pass the time, she often sat by the window and sang.

One day, a prince rode through the forest. Enchanted by the sound of Rapunzel's sweet voice, the young prince followed it until he came to the doorless tower.

Just then the witch arrived. The prince quickly hid as she called:
"Rapunzel, Rapunzel!
Let down your long hair!"

The witch began to climb the hair, and the prince knew that this was the way he would be able to meet the owner of the beautiful voice.

After the witch had gone, the prince stood beneath the tower and called in a voice like the witch's:

"Rapunzel, Rapunzel!
Let down your long hair!"

When Rapunzel's golden hair came tumbling down, he climbed up to the window.

Rapunzel was frightened when she saw the prince. But he was gentle and kind, and she quickly lost her fear.

The prince came to see Rapunzel often, and they soon fell in love. He asked her to marry him – but how would Rapunzel leave the tower?

Rapunzel had an idea. "Each time you visit," she told the prince, "bring me a ball of strong silk. I will plait it into a long, long ladder. When it is finished I will climb down and run away to marry you."

The prince did as Rapunzel asked, and soon the ladder was ready.

But on the very day she was to run away, something terrible happened. When the witch climbed through the window, Rapunzel absent-mindedly said, "Why do you pull so hard at my hair? The prince is not so rough." Suddenly, Rapunzel realised what she had said.

The witch flew into a raging fury. "You ungrateful little wretch!" she screamed. "I have protected you from the world, and you have betrayed me. Now you must be punished!"

"I'm sorry," Rapunzel sobbed, as she fell to her knees. "I didn't mean to make you cross."

The witch grabbed a pair of scissors and – snip-snap-snip-snap – cut off Rapunzel's long golden hair. Then, using the ladder to climb down, the witch carried Rapunzel off to a faraway land, where she left her to wander all alone without any food, water or anything to keep her warm.

That evening, when the prince called, the witch let down Rapunzel's hair. The prince climbed quickly up, and couldn't believe his eyes!

"The bird has flown, my pretty!" the witch cackled evilly. "You will never see Rapunzel again!"

Overcome with grief, the sad prince threw himself from the tower. His fall was broken by some brambles, but they also scratched and blinded him.

The prince stumbled away and wandered the land for a year, living on berries and rain water.

Then one day the prince heard a beautiful sound – the sweet voice of Rapunzel! He called her name and she ran into his arms, weeping tears of joy. The tears fell onto the prince's wounded eyes and suddenly he could see again.

The prince took his Rapunzel home to his castle, where they were married and lived happily ever after.